GINGER IN THE CITY

Written and Illustrated
by Jeannie Friedman

Copyright © MCMXCII Playmore Inc., Publishers
and Waldman Publishing Corp., New York, New York
All rights reserved
Printed in China

A young dog
named Ginger
lived in the
country. All day
long, she ran
in the grass.

...t all night long,
...e dreamed
...out life in the
..., busy city on
... other side
...he river.

And so, one day, brave Ginger packed her suitcase and moved across the river to the city where she'd always wanted to live.

The city was even
bigger than she had ever
dreamed…

...and she wanted to explore and see everything.

CAFE BOW WOW

TAXI

But in her apartment, Ginger was all alone.

"There's nobody here to talk to except me!" she thought. Then she had an idea. . .

"Maybe my next door neighbor is home. I'll knock once, just to say hello."

Just as she knocked, the door swung open, and there stood a giant yellow dog in a flowered robe.

"Hello, my name is Ginge(r)
and . . ." "Darling," sa(id)
out the yellow dog, "I'(m)
Dolly." And with a
whoosh of her great
paw, she swept
Ginger inside. Dolly
had all sorts of
doggie goodies, and
all night long, the
two neighbors talked
about the big city.

When Ginger got back to her own apartment, she didn't feel lonely any more. She knew she had made her first new friend.

Now Ginger had her new apartment and her first friend. What she needed next was a job.

Boom! She was hired by The Wagging Tail, the fanciest restaurant in town.

"I can't do this all alone!

Who ordered soup and who ordered bones!" wailed poor Ginger.

"No such word as can't," yipped Toni, a frisky white dog,

"Watch me!"

Ginger pushed back her ears, tied her apron tight, and copied everything the little white dog did — a bit slower, but she did it.

"I knew you could do it," yipped Toni. And Ginger knew she had made her second friend.

That weekend Ginger went to exercise class. All the dogs were lined up, stretching and stepping and showing their muscles.

"Will I ever be able to do all that?" Ginger wondered.

But Mona Bona, the exercise teacher, took her aside and showed her how to begin. Soon Ginger was moving just like all the other dogs in the class. She learned all the routines very quickly, but best of all, she knew she had made another friend.

Before long Ginger was running with the pack. Jogging along, singing a song — what a great way to see the city.

There was so much to do in the big city. The next week, Ginger went to art class.

"Excuse me," she asked shyly, "but how do I mix the color green?"

A large gray dog painting beside her squeezed a dab
of blue and a dab of yellow onto a piece of white paper.
When she mixed the two together, there was green.

The gray dog's name was Bonnie,
and she knew a lot about art.

With Bonnie's help, Ginger thought, soon she'd know a lot about art, too. How much she was learning from all her big city friends.

Enough to make all the colors of the rainbow. Enough
to thank all her friends for their help.

The next week, Ginger phoned Dolly, Toni, Mona Bona, and Bonnie to invite them to a party.

"Bring all your other friends, too," she told them.

The dogs had fun late into the night. They played games, they danced in circles, they told riddles, and ate some snacks.

The next Saturday night, they all had a pajama party.

When Ginger went to sleep,
she had never been happier. Life
in the big city was even better than
it had been in her dreams.